LITTLE TURTLE

ALLEN COUNTY PUBLIC LIBRARY
3 1833 01165 1194

W9-BYK-375

JE
Robbins, Ken.
Beach days
L 7135473

WITHDRAWN

DO NOT REMOVE
CARDS FROM POCKET

ALLEN COUNTY PUBLIC LIBRARY
FORT WAYNE, INDIANA 46802

You may return this book to any agency, branch,
or bookmobile of the Allen County Public Library.

DEMCO

Beach Days

BEACH DAYS

TEXT AND PHOTOGRAPHS BY KEN ROBBINS

Viking Kestrel

ABOUT THE PICTURES

All the photographs in this book were shot in black and white, printed on lifospeed black and white paper, and hand-colored by the author, using watercolor dyes. They were taken in the summer of 1986 in East Hampton, New York, and on Nantucket Island, off the coast of Cape Cod.

VIKING KESTREL
Viking Penguin Inc., 40 West 23rd Street, New York, New York 10010, U.S.A.
Penguin Books Ltd, Harmondsworth, Middlesex, England
Penguin Books Australia Ltd, Ringwood, Victoria, Australia
Penguin Books Canada Limited, 2801 John Street, Markham, Ontario, Canada L3R 1B4
Penguin Books (N.Z.) Ltd, 182-190 Wairau Road, Auckland 10, New Zealand

Copyright © Ken Robbins, 1987
All rights reserved
First published in 1987 by Viking Penguin Inc.
Published simultaneously in Canada
Printed in Hong Kong by Imago Publishing Ltd.
Jacket printed in U.S.A.
Set in Benguiat Book.
1 2 3 4 5 91 90 89 88 87

Library of Congress Cataloging in Publication Data
Robbins, Ken. Beach days.
Summary: Hand-tinted photographs and simple, poetic text re-create the fun of a beach trip.
[1. Beaches—Fiction] I. Title.
PZ7.R5327Day 1987 [Fic] 86-28129 ISBN 0-670-80138-0

Without limiting the rights under copyright reserved above, no part of this publication may be reproduced, stored in or introduced into a retrieval system, or transmitted, in any form or by any means (electronic, mechanical, photocopying, recording or otherwise), without the prior written permission of both the copyright owner and the above publisher of this book.

For Miles O'Brien

Allen County Public Library
Ft. Wayne, Indiana

L 7135473

Not every day is a beach day, though the beach is always there. Often it's too cold, or the waves are too high, or you have to be somewhere else.

Sometimes it's raining, there's snow or there's sleet, and nobody thinks of the beach.

But sometimes it's perfect—school's out, surf's up, the sun is high, the air is warm...then everyone heads for the beach.

Some people come all by themselves,

Some bring the whole family and more…

Surfboards, rafts and innertubes,

Beach balls, and kites.

Some prefer an empty beach,

Some love the crowds.

Some build a castle,

Some dig in the sand.

Some have hot dogs,

Some ice cream.

Some walk,

Some run.

Some test the water at the edge of the surf,

Some jump right in.

Some people like to ride the waves.

Some try to catch the wind.

F2
F2

Some watch the fishing boats go by,

Some sail their own.

Some play games,

Some float around all day.

And some just come to sit and watch...

The greatest show on earth.

ACKNOWLEDGMENTS

First of all, thanks to Maria, who deserves more credit than she's getting; thanks to Miles and Kate O'Brien, Lily Henderson, Elizabeth Strachan, Sam Taylor, Andy Friedman, Zack Allentuck, Shara Friend, Elizabeth De Sario, Zachary De Sario, Jesse Rosenthal, and Aja DeKeleva Cohen for their splendid efforts on behalf of this book; thanks to their parents, too; and special thanks to John and Antoinette. K.R.